The Adventures of the Organic Animal Club

The Adventures of the Organic Animal Club

E.L. Goodwin

authorHOUSE®

AuthorHouse™
1663 Liberty Drive
Bloomington, IN 47403
www.authorhouse.com
Phone: 1 (800) 839-8640

Published by AuthorHouse   12/01/2015

ISBN: 978-1-5049-6390-9 (sc)
ISBN: 978-1-5049-6389-3 (e)

Library of Congress Control Number: 2015919425

Print information available on the last page.

CONTENTS

This book is dedicated to my father and mother, who showed me how to plant trees, gardens, and flowers. It is also dedicated to my grandfather, who left us on Earth Day. It is also dedicated to parents who show their children to love and respect our planet with green, healthy, and organic ways.

CHAPTER 1

The Organic Animal Club Begins

Bert Bear was brown bear. He got a little bit bigger in the winter when he hibernated and ate more, as all bears do. Generally, he ate the wrong things, foods with too much salt and sugar. He did not realize that he ate things that were overly processed, such as frozen pizza and store-bought cookies. He ate cinnamon-sugar- donuts and too many of them. Also, he drank a lot of soda and ate candy. Sometimes, he did not enough vegetables or get any exercise.

Sometimes his tummy would hurt from all the gluten and wheat he ate at times in the pizza and cookies. He did not know why though. He just knew that after this year after all the television watching he had done on the couch, his pants did not fit and were too tight.

His best friend was Fred Fox, a red fox. Fred Fox was in tip-top shape because he was out and about all winter long, scooting across the snow. He was always on the move, jogging along the trails, and he always shopped at the organic farm market with their friend Olivia Owl. The market was held inside in the winter and moved outside in the summer.

Fred Fox made delicious gluten-free homemade veggie pizzas. Bert Bear liked the way those tasted, but he did not know how to make them or cook that much either. Bert Bear was always on the couch watching television when Fred Fox and Olivia Owl went to the farmers' market anyhow. They were both in good shape, felt well. and seemed healthy. Though, Olivia Owl had an autoimmune condition and was highly allergic to certain foods like soy and peanuts, as well as indoor and outdoor allergens.

Olivia Owl always said, "Fresh is best," when she brought Bert Bear food or had him to dinner.

"Maybe Olivia Owl is right," thought Bert Bear. "Maybe fresh is best."

Toward the end of winter, as Bert Bear slowly woke from hibernation, he noticed that he often sat on the sofa too long watching movies and playing video games. He was not terribly physically active either. In addition, eating frozen pizza and drinking soda made him feel more sluggish. It was a vicious cycle of eating and sleeping on the couch instead of getting fresh food and fresh air.

Bert Bear noticed that he had gained weight when he tried on his spring pants. They did not fit quite right. He was thinking about going for a walk since the sun had come out, and he had read about the benefits of vitamin D and sunshine.

Fred Fox came over to see Bert Bear and to bring him some salad and fresh berries. Bert Bear came out from the bedroom and showed Fred Fox his pants. His tummy was hanging out over the top.

"Isn't that what bears are supposed to do when they hibernate? Gain weight?" asked Bert Bear as he stood unhappily looking at his waist in the mirror.

Fred Fox was pretty clever, as all foxes are, and he knew not to directly answer the question, Bert Bear might get upset.

Instead, he said, "Maybe we should go outside and play instead of watching movies and playing video games all the time."

"I think you are right. No more pizza and soda. Or cookies. Or donuts," Bert Bear replied.

"I just went to the indoor farmers' market with Olivia Owl. I got you some salad greens and some fresh berries," Fred Fox said, showing him the reusable canvas tote bag on the table.

"Thank you. I want to make a salad later and get rid of all this processed food like you and Olivia Owl keep telling me," Bert Bear said. He was still looking at his tummy hanging over his pants.

"Fresh is best," Fred Fox said, smiling.

"I am beginning to realize that, and I want to go to the farmers' markets and learn more about organic and local foods instead of prepackaged, processed ones. I want my pants to fit, and I want to be healthier," Bert Bear explained.

"Plus, all the canned food that Rebecca Rabbit eats is controversial, with what is in the can linings and the link to cancer," Fred Fox said.

"Let's get outside, go explore, and get some fresh air. I need to start exercising regularly too, even if it is just walking," Bert Bear stated.

"Yes. Let's go for a nature walk," Fred Fox agreed.

"Okay. Grab your jacket, and let's go explore. I have to go on a diet and lose weight," Bert Bear said.

"Fresh air is good for the soul and the mind. You need to eat healthily as well to lose weight and eat the right things," Fred Fox stated.

"No more junk food. I want to be healthy and thinner!" Bert Bear exclaimed.

The pair jumped up and left Bert Bear's den for the fresh air and sunshine. It felt good to be off the sofa and away from the television to feel the wind and sunshine.

"This is the first time all winter I have been outside. I've been eating donuts on the couch," Bert Bear said.

"Well, let's start a new habit of being outside together and going exploring," Fred Fox said.

They headed down the path toward the woodlands up on the hill. The leaves were just about to open on the trees, and the air was free of pollen. Their friend Olivia Owl was very allergic to pollen, certain foods, and indoor allergens. She had a weaker immune system because of an autoimmune condition.

"Let's go by Olivia Owl's house and pick her up," said Bert Bear.

"Good idea. Let's go," said Fred Fox.

They turned off the path to the woodland area and went down the road to Olivia Owl's nest. They spotted her outside doing a spring cleanup with her broom. She looked as though she were going to sneeze from all the pollen.

"Hi, Fred Fox and Bert Bear!" Olivia Owl exclaimed as they came up the stone path. She was starting to sneeze, so she took out a tissue to blow her nose.

"Are you sick?" Fred Fox inquired of Olivia Owl.

"No, just seasonal allergies with the pollen about to burst in the trees and flowers," Olivia Owl replied. "You know how sensitive my immune system is to certain foods too. I have to get my immune system stronger with good, clean organic eating."

"Is that why you eat so healthily, do yoga, and exercise?" Bert Bear asked her.

"Yes, to keep my body pure, fresh, strong, and stress-free," Olivia Owl explained, putting her broom down.

"We're going exploring on a trail hike. Want to come?" Fred Fox asked Olivia Owl.

"Sure, let's go. I can show you where I pick berries and get some nuts and seeds for my salads and yogurt. But I can't eat peanuts or soy because I am allergic," Olivia Owl said.

"Your salads are always fresh and healthy, with or without peanuts," Fred Fox commented.

"I try to eat all organic, which means without pesticides. I like fresh produce from a garden or local farmers' market," Olivia Owl explained.

"What about if you have to go to the supermarket?" inquired Bert Bear.

"Most have organic sections," Olivia Owl stated.

"And you do yoga and walking for stress reduction," Fred Fox noted.

"I do it a few times a week because keeping free of stress keeps me healthy and strong," Olivia Owl replied.

Bert Bear was listening to this as they walked along the trail. He thought it would be a good idea for him to be in a healthy club to learn more and be healthier. He wanted to eat well, live a healthy life, and do so with his friends.

"Let's start a healthy kind of club to keep me on the right path, away from donuts, sugar, and junk food," Bert Bear said enthusiastically.

"What an organic idea," said Fred Fox with a coy smile.

"How about the Organic Animal Club?" Olivia Owl inquired happily.

"That's it. We are all officially in the Organic Animal Club," Bert Bear stated.

"We can eat healthy, do trail walks and yoga, help Olivia with her allergies, and maybe even grow a garden together," Fred Fox said with passion.

Fred Fox was relieved that after all the time he had spent trying to convince Bert Bear to eat better and exercise, Bert Bear finally wanted to try it. After all, new pants every year are expensive, even if they are not made of organic cotton which most affordable ones are not.

"You can learn about recycling and composting. Green living ties in with organic life too," Olivia Owl explained.

"What is composting?" asked Bert Bear.

"It is kind of like repurposing your refuse and trash. I put all of my organic trash such as potato peelings and apple that can decompose into my compost pile. I use it in my garden. I also recycle all of my metals, plastics, papers, and even my clothes in the proper bins at the town transfer station," explained Olivia Owl.

"That is why you hardly ever have any trash in your bins," stated Fred Fox.

"How do you recycle your clothes?" asked Bert Bear.

"I donate them so someone else may use them. Sometimes, I use them for another purpose, such as cutting them into cleaning rags if they are really old," explained Olivia Owl.

"I have to fit into my khakis and kick the sugar and junk food out of my diet. Having the club will motivate me more. Maybe I will get thin enough to recycle my khakis." Bert Bear was determined and thought more about organic and green living.

"There is a lot to learn, and we can all work together and find ways to be green, organic, and healthy." Olivia Owl said.

She was thrilled that her friend had awakened from the long winter and opened his eyes to the lifestyle she had embraced for most of her life. She always told her friends that it was better for their health to be organic and green. This lifestyle respected the planet for this generation and those to come.

"So, we just established the Organic Animal Club, and we will all work together to be green and organic," Olivia Owl said with a smile.

"It is organic and natural that we formed the club on our trail hike," joked Fred Fox.

"We can buy organic, eat organic, and be organic. We can be green, healthy, and lean," Olivia Owl stated.

"The label on my shirt said it is made of organic cotton. Is that good?" asked Fred Fox.

"Yes. That means that the cotton was not treated with harsh chemicals as it was grown and processed. This can make cotton cost more to produce, but it is worth it for you and the environment," Olivia Owl explained.

"I read that article you gave me about the pesticides and chemicals from conventional food and cotton getting washed into the streams and contaminating them," Fred Fox stated.

The three stopped to look at a stream that was running alongside the path. Bert Bear noted how pretty and clean the stream looked. The water was very clear and crisp. He stopped to reach down and touch it, and it was cold and refreshing.

"Look how clear the water is in the stream that runs through the woods. This is the same stream that runs by our houses and land," Bert Bear noted.

"It is clear and clean. It is important to preserve our water resources for us and future generations," Olivia Owl told them.

"What does it mean to clean with green? I heard you talk about that before," asked Fred Fox.

He had heard some of the earthy green lingo and started to read labels in the supermarket. He really thought it would be good to spend more time with Olivia Owl to learn more about being organic and green.

"Household and garden chemicals should be green because they can seep into the ground and water and into our bodies," Olivia Owl detailed.

"It seems as though there is a lot to learn, but it is all good for us and the planet. It is just about learning, being aware, and practicing green ideas." Bert Bear stated.

He wondered why he had never practiced all of these good things before, but he was thankful that he had been inspired and educated by Olivia Owl to do so now. He realized that not everyone had been educated on or raised with good environmental habits. He wanted to learn about them now so that he could start doing them now as well as pass them onto future generations.

"What a great day and a great club we started," Fred Fox said.

"Yes, and the more the merrier," Olivia Owl said.

She was thinking of their dear friend Rebecca Rabbit whom she had previously tried to encourage about green and organic ways. Olivia Owl had left her information to read about canned and processed foods, but it never seemed to make a difference for Rebecca Rabbit.

Rebecca Rabbit actually did some good environmental things, but was not fully committed. She did recycle her cans, and Olivia Owl was happy with that, but she wished could encourage Rebecca Rabbit more. She thought that Rebecca Rabbit would perhaps want to be a part of the Organic Animal Club and work to be more green and organic.

"Members just have to want to be healthy, green, and organic, and they can join the club," Bert Bear said.

"And hug trees for Earth Day at my Earth Day party," Olivia Owl said with a smile.

Olivia Owl had always been very natural and earthy. She had an Earth Day party for her friends every year to celebrate the planet. Bert Bear and Fred Fox had sometimes gone over the years, but they mostly went for the fresh-tasting food. Until now, Bert Bear had not known a lot about green and organic and helping the planet. Fred Fox had learned a lot from Olivia Owl, but he was glad that she had explained more to them today.

Her parents had instilled solid green and organic living from the start because she suffered from allergies and immune system issues. She had always eaten clean and fresh to minimize her symptoms. As she grew up, she learned to be more aware of the environment. She was more enthusiastic about it as she embraced this type of living, even more so as she got older and wanted to share it with others. Sharing is caring, and she cared about herself and the environment.

Every day, she realized small things that made a difference. These were small things such as recycling a plastic bag or container or using reusable bags at the market and grocery stores.

"If we all do one organic or green thing each day, it makes a difference not only for us, but also for our planet," Olivia Owl shared.

Bert Bear and Fred Fox always saw her recycle bottles, cans, papers, plastic, and metal as well as just about everything possible.

The three friends walked down the path toward the woodlands to explore together, delighted in becoming green and going organic.

It felt good to Bert Bear to get some exercise and stretch his legs. He felt good to be off the sofa and away from the television and junk food. Fresh air filled his body, mind, and soul. He noticed some spring flowers budding on the hillside, and the cinnamon donut did not seem as appealing. He was excited about the Organic Animal Club and felt healthier already because of his inspiration and education. Going green and organic was going to be an adventure.

CHAPTER 2

Allergies and Labels

The three friends continued down a wide dirt path into the nearby woodlands. There were some flowers popping up. Birds were fluttering, and bees were humming and buzzing around their heads.

Bert Bear asked, "Where can I get some fresh honeycomb? That is better than a cinnamon donut, right?"

"It is probably a better sugar than a donut because it is natural," Olivia Owl answered with a smile. She sneezed again and wiped her nose with a tissue from her pocket.

"You are allergic to pollen, which is an outdoor allergen, right?" asked Bert Bear.

"Yes. I am allergic to indoor allergens too, such as mold spores and dust mites," Olivia Owl said. "Actually, I eat local honey to fortify my immune system," Olivia Owl explained. She did not like to take a lot of medications unnecessarily and embraced natural methods too."

Ever since Olivia Owl was a little girl, she had had allergies to indoor things. She also had food allergies to peanuts, soy, and gluten. She stopped eating a lot of processed foods because of their ingredients.

Her immune system was sensitive, and she even had seasonal allergies. Through this adversity, she learned to eat pure, fresh, organic, and simple to minimize these symptoms the best she could. It gave her more awareness about organic and clean eating, and she wanted to share her knowledge with her friends in their new club.

Fred Fox reached in his shirt pocket and pulled out a trail mix bar. He always brought one along for a quick snack. He thought it was better than a candy bar and had been telling Bert Bear about switching to those too. Olivia Owl made her own granola bars from scratch and sometimes shared them with Fred Fox.

"Anyone want to split my bar?" Fred Fox asked. He offered it to Bert Bear and Olivia Owl.

"Does it have peanuts?" asked Olivia Owl.

She was a label reader. Anything with peanuts was off her list, as was anything manufactured in a facility that handled peanuts. Most often, she made her own trail bars at home so she knew exactly what was in them. She cooked at home nearly all the time unless there was a good organic restaurant.

"Let me read the label and see," said Fred Fox.

He got out his glasses and stopped to read the label. It did not have peanuts, soy, or gluten.

"I think you can have a bite, Olivia Owl, because it does not have anything you are allergic to, and it is not processed in a facility that had them there either," Fred Fox stated.

"In the old days, all food was organic and not processed," proclaimed Olivia Owl.

"I want to be organic and eat unprocessed foods too," Bert Bear said with a smile.

"So, let's share the trail bar and have a quick snack while we walk back," Fred Fox said.

"So this was our first adventure," Bert Bear said.

"We should have another one soon and go to the farmers' market with Bert Bear," Olivia Owl determined.

"I like going for the fresh organic local foods," Fred Fox announced.

"I like shopping local," Olivia Owl said.

Shopping local supports your local area business, and she believed in doing that to fortify not only herself as well as her community.

"I want to go and see what is there too," Bert Bear said.

"Let's go next week," Fred Fox said.

"I love the market in town. Shop local and buy fresh direct from the farm to table. I am all about that," Olivia Owl said.

"Support your local farmer and business," Fred Fox mused.

"Without farms, there is no food. Remember that. I even have a small garden out back for herbs and vegetables," said Olivia Owl.

"Bring your own canvas bag or tote so you don't have to use a plastic or paper bag when you shop," Olivia Owl suggested. She had a few canvas totes that she carried with her to the market or stores. That way, she had fewer plastic bags to recycle or dispose of.

She adored gardening. She had always wanted to make a community garden in their neighborhood so that her friends could work together to share in the bounty of what they grew. Some neighborhoods had that, and it worked well because everyone worked together to enjoy the harvest. It would be wonderful to have a big garden with her friends and work on it together.

"What do they do at the farmers' market?" Bert Bear asked.

"Farmers come and sell their fresh organic produce or local products. There's no middleman like there is at the big supermarket where you shop for your donuts," Olivia Owl answered with a smile.

"Where I formerly shopped for donuts," Bert Bear reminded her. He was really encouraged today to take the step to join in the environmentally correct life with green, organic, and healthy ways.

"The farmers work so hard to bring fresh produce to our tables all year long," Fred Fox explained.

"It is all non-GMO," Olivia Owl explained.

"GMO?" asked Bert Bear.

"Genetically modified organisms. Some produce is allowed to be genetically modified or changed like soy, tomatoes, cotton seeds, corn, and beets. I don't want that in my body. I read all the labels and read where produce comes from. Other countries allow more liberal use of pesticides on produce, and you have to be careful about that," Olivia Owl said emphatically.

Olivia Owl was well educated in organic and green. Bert Bear was listening carefully to everything. He planned to research all of these subjects more. He wanted to be a good green bear.

"You want to look for labels that say non-GMO," said Olivia Owl.

"Maybe we should start our own garden and grow our own vegetables," suggested Fred Fox.

That was garden music to Olivia Owl's ears.

"I have always wanted to do that with you and my good friends," Olivia Owl said.

"Let's go to the market and see what it sells. Then, let's start our own garden," suggested Fred Fox.

He was eager to have healthy vegetables and had watched Olivia Owl grow her small herb and vegetable garden. Maybe if they all worked together, they could grow different things and share them.

"We can make our own community garden and work together. We can share the produce we grow," stated Olivia Owl.

"I can't wait to go to the market together," Bert Bear said.

"Want to see if Rebecca Rabbit is home and ask her to join our club?" Olivia Owl asked. She thought maybe the three of them could persuade her to join them and go more green and organic.

"Rebecca Rabbit eats only canned carrots," explained Fred Fox. Rebecca Rabbit is was a beige rabbit who lived right next to Bert Bear.

"Remember my motto: Fresh is best!" Olivia Owl enthusiastically said.

"Let's go to her house and ask her to join our club and work in the community garden," Fred Fox said.

"She does some good environmental things such as recycle her cans, and I think she wants to do more, but she does not know how or what exactly. I leave her articles to read, but I don't ever hear back from her about them," Olivia Owl said, sneezing again into her tissue.

"Even though you have allergies, it is great to be outdoors together with you today to get vitamin D. I read the article you left me on that and all its benefits," Bert Bear said.

"So, our trail walk is better than watching TV on the couch?" mused Fred Fox.

"Yes, I like stretching my legs and getting some fresh air. Maybe my spring khaki pants will fit better soon, and I will be a skinny, healthy, organic, green bear," Bert Bear said with a smile.

The three friends walked back toward their neighborhood and Rebecca Rabbit's house. This was their first real adventure as the Organic Animal Club, and they all appreciated Olivia Owl's information and wanted to be healthy together.

CHAPTER 3

Membership Drive

After the long nature hike in the woodlands, the three friends made it to Rebecca Rabbit's. They walked up her path and knocked on her door.

"Who is it?" asked Rebecca Rabbit. She opened the door and saw her three friends.

"Thought we'd stop by after our trail walk and see if you want to join our new club," said Bert Bear proudly.

"You? On a trail walk and nature hike?" mused Rebecca Rabbit, looking Bert Bear up and down.

"Yes. I went on a long hike today, and we started a new club," stated Bert Bear.

"Suddenly, you are eating better and working out and hiking?" replied Rebecca Rabbit.

"I am, and we are" Bert Bear replied, referring to Fred Fox and Olivia Owl.

"What club are you talking about?" inquired Rebecca Rabbit.

Rebecca Rabbit invited them to come in and sit at her kitchen table. Her kitchen table was covered with canned carrots. She had just returned from the big supermarket and had yet to put them in her pantry. Folded paper bags from the store on the table. Sometimes, she saved them for the next time she needed a paper bag. She always did recycle her cans though at the town transfer station.

"I am talking about the Organic Animal Club we just started today. Want to join?" Bert Bear asked.

"We eat organic and healthy, exercise, and might want to make a community garden together," Fred Fox described.

"Basically, we want to live a green and organic life," Olivia Owl described.

"I can't afford organic or green or yoga or all of that," Rebecca Rabbit continued. "And I don't know how to garden alone or in a community."

"We can learn together from Olivia Owl, who is already living organic and green with her allergies and autoimmune condition" Fred Fox explained, encouraging Rebecca Rabbit to try the Organic Animal Club.

"Eating processed food is not good for you in the long run, and canned things have controversial long-term issues," explained Olivia Owl.

She had left Rebecca Rabbit articles and information on the organic life over the years to try to inform her about various topics.

"Fresh organic carrots are healthier than processed," Fred Fox told Rebecca Rabbit.

"I don't know how to cook and store them for winter, and from what I hear, it is a lot of work to be organic," replied Rebecca Rabbit,

"Well, you can come with us to do yoga this week or go on a trail hike and be part of our club," Olivia Owl said.

"Maybe Olivia Owl can teach you how to cook the fresh carrots and store them," Fred Fox explained to Rebecca Rabbit.

"I can't do yoga. I can't cook, and I don't want to join your club because organic is too expensive for me," Rebecca Rabbit explained.

She was very thrifty and budget conscious and shopped at only thrift stores. Actually, she did not realize that she was already living a sort of green lifestyle by doing that. She purchased some recycled goods and clothing that someone would have otherwise tossed in the garbage. That felt good to her not just for economic reasons but also for the planet. She was not entirely opposed to being environmentally correct, green, or organic. She just thought it was too expensive in time, cost, and effort.

"I respect the planet. But I eat my canned carrots and don't do trail hikes or yoga" Rebecca Rabbit reiterated.

"You won't join our club?" Bert Bear asked with disappointment.

Rebecca Rabbit showed them all of her canned carrots and said, "No, I won't join your new club."

"Bert Bear and Fred Fox are going to grow a garden with me," Olivia Owl mentioned.

"Why grow a garden when you can just eat canned carrots?" asked Rebecca Rabbit.

"Organic and fresh is best. All the good nutrients are in fresh, unprocessed foods," Olivia Owl explained.

"Well, I don't have the rabbit funds to buy fresh and organic. I don't have the energy to work in the garden. The farmers' market is only once a week, and I am usually busy that day. I buy canned," Rebecca Rabbit told them. She was making a lot of excuses.

"Fresh things cost less than canned, and you will see, Rebecca Rabbit, if you come with me to the farmers' market," Olivia Owl tried to explain.

"Work on the garden with us at least?" Fred Fox asked.

"Too much work for me. Just need my carrots in the can." Rebecca Rabbit said.

"I hope you recycle your cans and do what is good for the planet by being green," Olivia Owl said to Rebecca Rabbit.

"I do what I can. It is a lot of work to do that, but I try," Rebecca Rabbit replied.

Because of the information Olivia Owl had left her to read, she tried to do small things within her day to be good for the earth such as recycling cans and buying secondhand clothing.

"Well, even if you don't want to be in our club, you are still our friend. Maybe, one day, you will join officially," Fred Fox said, and all the animals agreed.

The three founding members of the Organic Animal Club agreed to start a community garden the next warm day that they had. Actually, Olivia Owl decided that Earth Day would be a good starting day for the garden. Earth Day is a day to do something good for the planet, and starting a garden just seemed right.

"Earth Day is a day to respect the planet. I think we should plan to start our garden that day, so that we can do something good for the planet," Olivia Owl suggested.

"I know about Earth Day. Let's plant our vegetables then," agreed Fred Fox.

"Earth Day sounds good to me," Bert Bear declared.

He had heard of Earth Day and doing something good for the planet at Olivia Owl's Earth Day parties. This included such things as planting trees and restoring the planet. Recycling was good because limiting trash helped. Not using pesticides was another good thing, as was avoiding toxic chemicals and fertilizers. Maybe just informing and educating a friend about good green habits would make a difference.

Bert Bear and Fred Fox knew that their friend had a lot of information for them about green and organic living. Olivia Owl used organic, nontoxic green cleaners in her house. Eating organic helped the farmers who grew organic produce have more demand to produce more. Buying organic clothing was also a positive thing. She also rode her bicycle or walked wherever she could to save gas and minimize pollution. There were lots of things to consider.

Rebecca Rabbit decided it was too much work for her, and she wanted to shop at her regular market and buy the cans of carrots. It occurred to her that if she did not stockpile so many cans in her pantry because they were on sale, she might be able to afford fresh carrots more often. She did not know how to cook and store them, though. No one had ever showed her how.

"How about it, Rebecca Rabbit? How about you join us in the garden on Earth Day and plant with us and join our club?" Bert Bear asked joyfully.

"I won't start a garden with you, but I will watch you from my window while I eat my canned carrots," joked Rebecca Rabbit with a smile.

"Yes, a garden takes time and work apparently," Fred Fox said with a sigh, looking out Rebecca Rabbit's kitchen window toward the flat grass area that joined all of their land. He thought that land would make a good spot for their new community garden.

"Especially having an organic garden with the composting we will have to do to fertilize it naturally and make the soil rich," Olivia Owl explained.

To build a compost pile near the shed, all the members of the Organic Animal Club would have to pile up their banana peels, coffee grounds, orange peels, lettuce, and anything else that could decompose naturally. Those types of things would help fertilize the soil. Plastic, metal, and similar things would not go into the compost pile.

"We can put all our compost pile near the toolshed, and when we are ready to grow the garden, it will be ready to use," Olivia Owl explained.

"Composting sounds like a lot of work. But it helps the planet since it creates less trash, so that sounds good," Bert Bear replied.

"We can also collect rain water in the big old bathtub behind the shed and use it for water for the garden," Olivia Owl said. Years ago, someone had left that old iron bathtub outside when they changed a bathroom around. Instead of hauling it to the refuse station, Olivia Owl thought it would make a good planter for flowers or a good rain collector for water. The bathtub, she explained, was an example of repurposing, reusing, and recycling.

"Well, after all this work, we can relax after and do some yoga," Olivia Owl answered.

"Not me," Rebecca Rabbit answered.

"Good for your mind, body, and soul," Fred Fox added.

"My mind, body and soul are staying in this kitchen and eating my canned carrots until further notice," stated Rebecca Rabbit.

"We should make a flyer and post it at the farmers' market to recruit other members for our club." Fred Fox suggested.

Bert Bear understood now how easy it was to go green and organic. After all, anyone can start a club where members can join and share for free. Sharing really is caring. Sharing information that is good for you and for the environment is a good, green thing.

"Good idea. Let's share it with other animals who want to be healthy with us, even if Rebecca Rabbit won't join now," Bert Bear said, looking at Rebecca Rabbit and all her canned processed carrots.

He thought that maybe she would join them someday. If Olivia Owl informed her about more about things, perhaps Rebecca Rabbit would consider it and really embrace the lifestyle.

"Tomorrow, we are going to try some yoga with Olivia Owl at her house," Bert Bear said.

"Maybe you want to come try it with us?" Fred Fox asked.

"Tomorrow, I have plans to watch movies all day inside," Rebecca Rabbit said definitively.

"How about coming with us to the farmers' market tomorrow?" Fred Fox asked.

"I think it will be the first day it will be outside this year, and it will be a nice one. You can walk with us and see all the vegetables," Olivia Owl stated.

"Probably not tomorrow," Rebecca Rabbit replied.

Olivia Owl was disappointed to hear that. However, she hoped that Rebecca Rabbit would try it with them one day. She was not going to push her. Sometimes, things take time. Olivia Owl realized that and respected Rebecca Rabbit's decision. It was hard to make big lifestyle changes, but maybe they could open her mind to it in time with more education and information.

Chapter 4

The Farmers' Market

The next day, the three members of the Organic Animal Club got ready to go to the farmers' market in town. Fred Fox had his straw basket ready, and he gave Bert Bear a big canvas tote to use for his purchases. Olivia Owl had a canvas tote as well as a basket because she usually bought a lot.

The farmers' market was spread out in the parking lot near the library. This was the same library where Rebecca Rabbit sometimes went to get her books. Once Olivia Owl ran into her there coming out of the library with her books, but Rebecca Rabbit was on her way to the supermarket to buy her canned carrots and would not stop to walk around the farmers' market.

The farmers' market was held once a week in the same spot outside in the nice weather days and months. If it rained or the weather was cold, many towns held farm markets indoors at various alternate locations like a greenhouse. Nearby towns had them on different days of the week with similar farmers and vendors. It was nice to be able to shop at various markets on different days.

There were many white tents to protect the farmers and their products from the sun. Each stand had a big table with a sign indicating the name of the farm. All the vegetables on the table were organized and priced to make shopping easy.

"I love walking around the farmers' markets because it is exercise. You don't even realize it because it is fun to be here walking around," Olivia Owl explained.

"Can't wait to get some fresh organic vegetables to roast with my organic olive oil," Fred Fox said.

"Can we come over for dinner and have some?" Bert Bear asked.

"Of course. We can even go vegetarian tonight with fava beans or peas for protein," Fred Fox said.

"Wow. You really have been paying attention and educating yourself," Olivia Owl replied.

"Maybe even some raw milk cheese for an appetizer," Fred Fox said.

Raw milk was unpasteurized and had fewer chemicals than conventional milk. You had to be cautious with everything, though, even the raw milk and read about things and make your best decisions for yourself. However, all foods were raw before processing started, according to what Fred Fox had read.

"Educating yourself and doing your own research helps the environment and the green and organic lifestyle," Fred Fox explained to Bert Bear.

They walked around the market together and looked at the various tables of foods and produce.

"You don't have to agree with everything you read or are told about the organic lifestyle. Just keep your mind open to it," Fred Fox said.

"Unlike Rebecca Rabbit," Bert Bear said.

"She is open to it, but it is taking her more time to see that she is already doing little things such as recycling and buying vintage clothes," Olivia Owl said.

"Maybe she will come around in time and join the Organic Animal Club," Fred Fox said hopefully.

"Look at the great tomatoes at this table," Olivia Owl said.

Bert Bear looked the different sizes and colors of the tomatoes. He had had never seen such fresh tomatoes.

He asked, "Why are they so different in size and color from each other?"

"Because they are not genetically modified to look the same," Olivia Owl said.

"I want some of those for my salad greens. I will bring a salad tonight to Fred Fox's house," said Bert Bear.

Bert Bear bought some tomatoes. Fred Fox filled his basket up with fresh vegetables to roast with his organic olive oil. He was still looking around from some fresh peas and fava beans for protein as well as some cheese.

"Look at all the fresh vegetables, cheese, and products here are labeled as organic" Olivia Owl stated.

"This is a fun way to shop, being outside and walking around from tent to tent," Bert Bear said.

"I know. I wish Rebecca Rabbit would come with us instead of being at home or sitting in the library with her books all the time," Fred Fox said.

"Maybe she will come to dinner tonight at your house," Bert Bear said hopefully.

"Tonight at dinner, I want to talk to you about stress levels and doing yoga in addition to walking," Olivia Owl explained.

"Sounds like a healthy plan with a healthy farm-to-table dinner," Fred Fox said.

"What is a farm-to-table dinner?" Bert Bear asked.

"Eating literally from a farm at your table," Fred Fox detailed.

"Without any food being processed or stored in cans or things like that," Olivia Owl explained.

"Let's find the organic cheese and some beans, and let's go to my house and cook this all up together as the first supper of the Organic Animal Club," Fred Fox suggested.

"Then we will do yoga tomorrow and talk more about our club," Olivia Owl said.

"I don't think Rebecca Rabbit will be able to come tonight because she was going to be at the library again," Fred Fox said.

"Yes. She is always there. I don't know what she is reading up on," Olivia Owl said.

"Well, this will be our first club supper. It is okay if she does not come. Maybe she can come next time, or we can cook something for her," Bert Bear stated.

The Organic Animal Club enjoyed the afternoon walking around at the farmers' market together. They supported the local farmers and businesses and got healthy, fresh, and organic foods to cook at Fred Fox's house. It was a very organic day, and they were happy they had started the club. They would have to work hard to convince Rebecca Rabbit to join them or think of a way to share more with her.

CHAPTER 5

Yoga for Three

The next day, Olivia Owl invited Fred Fox and Bert Bear to her house to tour her yoga studio. It was very bright, and there were yoga mats and pretty windows that opened to views of the woodlands. It was very meditative and relaxing.

The three friends gazed out at the studio and remarked together about healthy lifestyles and how important it was to eat right and have an activity to remove stress from your life. Exercise does not have to be expensive or at a gym or a club. Olivia Owl learned it at home from videos from the library as well as ones online and set up her own studio. Walking is free exercise, as is gardening. The Organic Animal Club tried to explain that to Rebecca Rabbit, but she was not yet ready to listen.

"I had this yoga studio put in the house so I did not have to keep up my gym membership and could spend more on healthy living to heal my allergies. I am trying to heal my body naturally as well as with medicine. Yoga is just part of a healthy lifestyle for your mind, body, and soul," explained Olivia Owl.

"I wish Rebecca Rabbit would give it a chance and see that you can exercise anywhere for free," Fred Fox said.

"Maybe if we do yoga outside near the garden this summer, she will see us from her kitchen window and want to join," Olivia Owl added.

"Maybe she will take a walk with us and join the Organic Animal Club," Bert Bear said.

"How about if we all do some beginner yoga poses now? I will show you what I have learned," said Olivia Owl.

"Let's start some yoga," Fred Fox answered.

"Okay. Let's get seated on our mats, and I will turn on some soft, relaxing music," Olivia Owl said.

"Rebecca Rabbit is missing out on the club and the yoga," Bert Bear said.

"She is such a doubter. Exercise does not have to be expensive. She already recycles and buys vintage clothes, but she does not realize she is partly living green," Fred Fox described.

"You are right. Exercise is free, just like our nature hike outside today. We don't have to be at a gym or expensive club. The outdoors can be your gym," Bert Bear noted.

"Or a friend who teaches you yoga. It is good to share a healthy lifestyle. Sharing really is caring," Olivia Owl explained with a smile.

Olivia Owl had Bert Bear sit in front of her and Fred Fox as she led their yoga session. The three practiced various beginner forms of meditation, stretches, and yoga poses. They breathed in deeply and exhaled slowly.

It was just a small start to open their minds to the art and study of yoga. Like anything, it took time to learn. Olivia Owl was glad that Fred Fox and Bert Bear were open to trying and exploring yoga.

Afterward, the three friends sat at Olivia Owl's table. They drank mineral water with a small snack of organic granola and bananas.

Bert Bear had learned not only about himself but also about Rebecca Rabbit. She was not fully open to the organic lifestyle because of economic reasons and concerns about time and cooking. He felt badly that she could not have all the fresh carrots she wanted because she was frugal and budget conscious and did not want to learn to cook. Being budget conscious is a valid constraint for some people who can't afford organic produce and want to have a healthier lifestyle.

Instead, he channeled those negative thoughts into positive actions. He had a plan to help her.

"Let's get our garden going soon. I want to get Rebecca Rabbit all the fresh carrots she can eat," Bert Bear said with hope.

"I want to teach her how to cook the carrots and store them for winter," Olivia Owl said.

"Let's go to the farmers' market and explore. Maybe we can start our own stand and sell our own vegetables together," Bert Bear said.

"What an organic idea," Olivia Owl said with delight.

"And I want to give her a job at the stand when we grow our vegetables and set up a shop at the local farmers' market. That way, she will have more money to buy organic carrots if she is willing to work with us," Fred Fox said.

"Plus, I will work hard and grow extra carrots for her," Bert Bear said.

"And I will teach her yoga and ask her to take trail hikes with us," Olivia Owl added.

The three friends made a plan to start their garden the next day which was Earth Day. Not only would this help themselves to set up the farm stand at the local farmers' market, but it would also help their friend Rebecca Rabbit be healthier.

CHAPTER 6

The Organic Earth Day Garden

The next day, on Earth Day, Olivia Owl, Fred Fox and Bert Bear decided on a spot to make their garden. The compost pile was ready to add to the soil to fertilize the vegetable seeds. Every day, members of the Organic Animal Club have been taking their fruits and vegetable scraps to the pile and safely covering them so that they make themselves into a nice sort of earthy stew full of nutrients. This was much better than conventional fertilizers.

"I am so glad we made the compost pile so we have natural fertilizer," Bert Bear said.

"We are what we eat, and I don't eat pesticides," Olivia Owl stated.

They selected a patch between Bert Bear's den and Rebecca Rabbit's hole. Rebecca Rabbit watched them for a while and then decided to go back into her house. The other animals really wished she would help them plant the garden.

It sunny, and the soil was fertile. They would not use any pesticides to grow organic vegetables. Olivia Owl explained that chemical pesticides and fertilizers can seep into the water and soil.

The garden got a lot of good sun, essential for growing good vegetables. It was also essential for animals and people to get enough sun and natural vitamin D while protecting from too much sun. Olivia Owl explained that they should all get sun in moderation, but that the vegetables needed it as much of it as they could, along with good rains to get the seeds started. The garden would also need to be watered if the rain didn't keep up adequately.

There was a large stream nearby that the animals could draw from to water the garden. Otherwise, they would hope for rain to come. Olivia Owl knew that it was best to water at sunset or early morning when the sun was not at its peak.

"Though the sun feels good on my body, I always wear my garden hat," explained Olivia Owl.

"I always wear my favorite plaid shirt to protect my arms and shoulders from the sun," said Fred Fox.

"Is it organic cotton?" asked Olivia Owl.

"Not sure. What is that?" asked Fred Fox.

"Organic cotton is not treated with chemicals as it grows," explained Olivia Owl.

"I wouldn't want unnecessary chemicals in my food or on my body," replied Fred Fox.

"Let's look into that," said Bert Bear. "I don't want the cotton my khakis are made of to be full of chemicals either."

"I always wear my sunglasses to protect my eyes because I am so sensitive to the sun after a long winter inside, I want to protect my eyes," Bert Bear said.

When they were ready to work on the garden, they had a system. They took string and outlined their garden from corner to corner with stakes in the ground before they got to work digging. It is important to square off your space, dig up the soil, turn it over, and chop it gently with the hoe and rakes. It was going to be a lot of work to dig the garden and plant the seeds.

"Once we get digging and planting, it is going to be a lot of work," Bert Bear assessed.

"Free exercise. Remember?" Fred Fox reminded him.

As Bert Bear stood there gazing out with a shovel in his hand, he sighed. It would be a lot of work to make the garden and start it, but the reward would be fresh vegetables and a healthy lifestyle. Plus, the Organic Animal Club was going to start a business at the local farmers' market.

All three friends had a good breakfast of oatmeal, berries, honey, and granola. They fortified themselves with healthy food before getting to work. They also had a lot of water and brought a big container with fresh lemons sliced in it so they could hydrate as they worked together.

They liked being outdoors together, working on something organic and good for them. The garden would be theirs, but they would share it. Bert Bear also knew that the carrots would go mostly to Rebecca Rabbit, and that made him hopeful and more eager to start planting.

"You are right, Olivia Owl. The sun feels good, and we need it to grow too. I spent too much time inside on the sofa with the television and donuts before. I was not outdoors walking, hiking, and planting a garden with my good friends," Bert Bear admitted.

"I feel better outdoors with my hands in the soil and planting the seeds," Fred Fox agreed.

After they squared off and dug up their garden, the three friends dug rows for seeds to be planted. They labeled each row of seeds. They grew spring peas, carrots for Rebecca Rabbit, tomatoes, potatoes, squash, onions, eggplant, and lettuce.

The garden was coming along as they raked, planted, and connected with the earth. The three friends laughed and shared just as much and more as they did inside in front of the television. They laughed even more because they were all dirty and tired. The wanted a good hearty dinner as earthy and nutritious as the soil and seeds they had worked with all day long.

"This was a long day planting, but I am so glad we have the garden ready to grow," Bert Bear said. "I can't wait to give the carrots to Rebecca Rabbit so she doesn't have to eat the canned ones anymore."

"I can't wait to make her the farm stand manager if she wants to do that job," exclaimed Fred Fox.

"I can't wait to help her cook and teach her yoga," Olivia Owl stated.

"Let's go get the watering cans and hoses now," Bert Bear suggested. He walked toward the toolshed.

"Or we can just pray for rain to fall into the old bathtub outside," laughed Fred Fox.

The three friends stood and stared in admiration at the garden they had planted. They all knew that fresh vegetables would soon grow and that they would be able to give the carrots to Rebecca Rabbit.

On Earth Day, the Organic Animal Club gave back to Mother Earth. They recycled their fruit and vegetable scraps into compost to naturally make the soil fertile. They planted a vegetable garden that would yield organic vegetables all summer long. They connected with the soil, sky, and planet. They remembered all who had been there before and all who would come to their garden and to this earth.

"Earth Day was the best day to plant the garden," Bert Bear stated.

"Let's start it every year on Earth Day," Fred Fox agreed.

"Let's go make a big salad and some homemade pea soup with what we bought at the farmers' market," Olivia Owl suggested.

"Let's invite Rebecca Rabbit over for dinner and see if she will consider joining the Organic Animal Club now," Olivia Owl suggested.

"Good idea. I will call her on my cell phone when I turn it back on. I like to disconnect every now and then," stated Fred Fox.

"I disconnect from my devices on weekends," said Olivia Owl in agreement.

The three headed for Olivia Owl's place to make a hearty organic salad and some warm pea soup. Fred Fox called Rebecca Rabbit, and she decided to join them. Rebecca Rabbit offered to bring dessert.

The three founding members of the Organic Animal Club were pleased with their day working outside and felt connected as friends as well as to the soil. They were excited to tell Rebecca Rabbit all about it. It was a good day to start the garden.

CHAPTER 7

Another Farm-to-Table Supper

Olivia Owl was a really good chef, especially when it came to farm-to-table cooking. It was easy for her to prepare simple and fresh dinners with fresh herbs and ingredients. She learned by trying recipes and making things that tasted fresh and simple.

Fred Fox and Bert Bear did not realize how satisfying fresh pea soup compared to its canned counterpart until they had tried it at Olivia Owl's house last winter.

"Rebecca Rabbit, you will have to try this pea soup," remarked Fred Fox. He worked with Bert Bear chopping the lettuce and other veggies after they had been washed.

"It is delicious and much better than pizza with all its calories and gluten. Gluten is not always bad for you unless you have an intolerance or disease like celiac disease or feel a sensitivity to it," remarked Bert Bear.

"I will try it because it has carrots in it," remarked Rebecca Rabbit.

"I will give you the recipe, Rebecca Rabbit, and we can make it together another time," Olivia Owl said.

Rebecca Rabbit watched her cook. The soup smelled good, and it was fresh. She knew that it had not been sitting on a shelf in the store like her canned carrots had. She smelled the fresh seasonings of all the ingredients from the farmers' market.

"We are going to set up a farm stand when the vegetables grow, Rebecca Rabbit," Bert Bear stated.

"Would you like to work at the farm stand and be our manager?" inquired Fred Fox.

"That way, we can work on the garden to get our vegetables there on time each week," added Bert Bear.

Rebecca Rabbit thought about it for one quick second and replied no. She was too busy playing her video games and watching television.

"I can't because I am busy," Rebecca Rabbit replied.

"Playing video games and watching television while we work in the garden," stated Fred Fox.

"Well, now that Bert Bear is part of the Organic Animal Club, I have no one to watch TV with or play video games with," added Rebecca Rabbit.

"You could make some money to buy fresh organic carrots if you worked with us," Bert Bear suggested.

"I like my canned carrots," Rebecca Rabbit said. She knew she preferred fresh cooked dinners like Olivia Owl was making for them tonight. The smell of the fresh peas, carrots, and herbs was so savory that she could not leave Olivia Owl's side at the stove.

"May I stir the soup?" asked Rebecca Rabbit.

"Why, of course you can," Olivia Owl replied happily. This was the first interest Rebecca Rabbit had shown.

Olivia Owl turned over her shoulder to smile at Bert Bear and Fred Fox, both of whom looked equally pleased at Rebecca Rabbit's interest. Just stirring it stirred up the notion in Rebecca Rabbit that organic and green were perhaps better choices for her.

"Look. I am being green, stirring my green soup," quipped Rebecca Rabbit.

"Now you have join our club," begged Bert Bear as he sliced tomatoes for the salad they would share.

"I won't join the club or work at your farm stand. Remember, I can't afford organic, and it takes too much work to make your garden grow. I watch you out the kitchen window," Rebecca Rabbit reminded them.

"How about a walk or some yoga tomorrow?" inquired Olivia Owl.

"I doubt it. I have to go the supermarket for more canned carrots," Rebecca Rabbit stated. She was still mesmerized as she stirred the big pot of pea soup with fresh carrots.

"Let's plate this delicious farm-to-table supper and share it as an Organic Animal Club supper," Olivia Owl suggested. She got out big soup bowls and salad plates.

"The salad is so fresh and light. I can't wait to eat it," declared Bert Bear.

"Never thought I would hear you say that," Fred Fox exclaimed with a smile.

"My khaki pants will fit better soon," said Bert Bear.

"What did you bring for dessert, Rebecca Rabbit?" asked Olivia Owl.

"Gluten-free, nut free brownies," Rebecca Rabbit said.

"Well, I will put out fresh fruit too," Olivia Owl politely added.

"Thank you for remembering and respecting that I try to eat gluten-free," Olivia Owl replied happily.

"Well, don't deprive yourself of a treat every once in a while," Fred Fox added.

"We worked it all off in the garden today, and a small indulgence for dessert is good too," remarked Bert Bear.

The friends sat down at Olivia Owl's table and shared their freshly tossed salad and hearty protein-rich pea soup with fresh carrots. It was so satisfying.

"When we harvest our own vegetables, we will make pea soup all the time," Olivia Owl stated.

Even Rebecca Rabbit savored the soup and salad. She really did love the fresh flavors of the food.

"I noticed some of your allergy symptoms have diminished since I have know you and you started eating pure and fresh, Olivia Owl," noted Bert Bear.

"You are what you eat. I am eating pure, fresh, and organic and feeling stronger. Yoga and walks as well as avoiding stress helps too," Olivia Owl replied.

"Then, I guess I am canned carrots," quipped Rebecca Rabbit with a smile.

"Not for long," mused Bert Bear. He knew that the fresh carrots soon would be ready for Rebecca Rabbit.

That night, the hearty and homey flavors of the simple soup warmed the kitchen. It also warmed Rebecca Rabbit a bit more to eating fresh carrots and learning to cook healthy suppers with her friends.

Maybe she would not buy as many new outfits from the vintage store and save more money for organic carrots. She noticed that Bert Bear fit into his khaki pants better and seemed more in shape since founding the Organic Animal Club. Olivia Owl was strong and healthy.

Fred Fox was thriving as he organized the club's business launch for the farm stand. It seemed that the Organic Animal Club was going smoothly. Maybe tomorrow she would not buy as many canned carrots at the supermarket. She would look around the garden or go to the farmers' market.

That night, Rebecca Rabbit thought about how delicious the food had tasted and how good she felt after eating it. It was not just the company of good friends. It was the fresh food and how it made her body feel. She had more energy and felt healthier than she did after eating her processed foods.

She did not realize that the act and art of cooking was just as meditative as yoga for the mind, body, and soul. There was a relaxation to taking the time to prepare the food together instead of just opening a can of carrots or soup. This was the real process that felt good to her, not the process of processed food.

When Olivia Owl served the gluten-free brownies, she served organic coffee too. She explained that anything can be organic, even chocolate or coffee. No pesticides were used in the production of them, but it was still good to always read labels for other ingredients one may be allergic to.

To Rebecca Rabbit, it seemed that she was getting a free education in the art of organic life from her friends. She could see differences in all of them. She realized that it was not a cure for anything. Rather, it seemed that the organic lifestyle was a good green choice that complemented their lives, and it seemed good to be included, at least for the pea soup supper that night.

CHAPTER 8

Repurpose, Recycle, and Reuse

Each Saturday, the Organic Animal Club loaded all of its refuse and trash in the red farm truck and hauled it to the recycling and transfer station center in town. The red farm truck had been tested for proper emissions and met the standards at the inspection station for pollution control. Bert Bear and Fred Fox had learned from Olivia Owl that is important to keep trash to a minimum.

Bert Bear said, "I can't believe that only a few months ago, I was sitting in front of my television eating pizza and donuts. Now, we have an organic farm-to-table garden and a farm stand at the farmers' market. I am even recycling."

"And your pants fit better, and you care about auto emission inspections for the red truck," joked Fred Fox as he unloaded all the cardboard.

"I don't even want the junk food anymore. I just want to make healthy choices, and I never thought I would say that," Bert Bear replied.

"With yoga, trail walks, and organic ways, you have become a better bear," mused Olivia Owl.

"A healthy and green bear," Bert Bear said, pleased with how he was feeling.

Bert Bear was in charge of the plastic and glass. Olivia Owl got the newspaper and paper. Some would be saved for their fireplaces for the winter, and most of their reading was online these days. That was the one green aspect of cell phones and devices. There was less paper. Taking things to the recycling center helped keep the planet green for the future

"You have taught us all a lot this season about being organic and healthy and about being green for our planet. It is all a connected lifestyle," Bert Bear added proudly. He was happy that he had shed his lifestyle of fast food, junk food, and inactivity for a much more green and organic lifestyle.

It was true that Olivia Owl had taught them all about gardening, healthy cooking, fresh vegetables, yoga, and trail walks. She had also informed Fred Fox and Bert Bear about being green and environmentally correct. That was not hard to do, and it felt good to recycle and repurpose things.

They recycled and reused bottles and plastics. They bought organic clothing shopped at thrift and vintage stores sometimes like Rebecca Rabbit did. There was a good feeling about living close to the earth and not being wasteful or toxic to the planet or themselves.

Olivia Owl had taught them the value of recycling and protecting the planet from too much trash. Plastic and paper bags were recycled the best they could. Most often, Olivia Owl used her canvas tote and taught Fred Fox and Bert Bear to do the same.

Rebecca Rabbit did have a recycle bin where she collected all of her carrot cans. The three really encouraged her to join their club because she did more than she realized to be green and organic.

Bert Bear and his friends also worked at composting for their organic garden as Olivia Owl had taught them. They put old fruits, vegetables, and even coffee grinds in a pile that would decompose into material that would nurture their garden. There was no need for traditional fertilizers in this garden.

"All of our actions will help save the planet for future generations" stated Olivia Owl.

"I am proud to be organic and green," said Bert Bear.

"Oh, look. It is Rebecca Rabbit recycling her carrot cans at the metal bin," Fred Fox said.

"We don't have metal because we don't eat from cans," Bert Bear added with a smile.

"Let's go over and help her since she has so much. Soon, we can give her fresh carrots. She won't need the cans then, but it is good she recycles now," Olivia Owl stated.

"Yes, tomorrow, we will harvest a lot of the garden and get the carrots ready. I can't wait," Bert Bear said as he headed over to help Rebecca Rabbit.

As he walks up to her, he asked her, "Got carrots?" with a smile.

Rebecca Rabbit turned to face him and said, "No, but I have plenty of cans I am recycling."

She was more green than she admitted to and more organic than she knew. Hopefully, she would fully join the Organic Animal Club one day.

CHAPTER 9

Harvesting the Garden

The sun and rain had done their jobs, and the garden was growing and ready for harvest. The Organic Animal Club had made sure to weed and water it and organically fertilize it with the compost Olivia Owl had taught them to make.

Every day, after a trail walk, they would work in the garden together. They looked forward to it. They protected it from bugs and insects with organic means.

It was a lot of work, but it was no more than any garden is. Each of the three friends took turns picking and putting vegetables in the wheelbarrow to bring to the farmers market in town. To see the bounty of what they grew was reward enough. To share it with other customers was a different reward entirely.

Fred Fox was in charge of the finances for the farm stand. Bert Bear did the farm stand set up and delivery. Olivia Owl handled selling the produce to the customers. However, she would have preferred to have been working in the garden.

"I wish Rebecca Rabbit would join our club and work as the manager at the farm stand," said Olivia Owl.

"We really could use her so we could grow more vegetables. It is not about the profit or money. Rather, it is the sharing of our organic produce with locals that is rewarding." Fred Fox stated proudly.

"Sharing is caring at the Organic Animal Club, and I want to share our carrots with Rebecca Rabbit very soon," Bert Bear reminded them.

Bert Bear always checked the carrots to make sure they were growing well. They were just about ready to be harvested, and he couldn't wait to give them to Rebecca Rabbit. Bert Bear had put special care into each carrot.

"I think we will give the carrots to Rebecca Rabbit tomorrow," Bert Bear determined.

"Great. Then I will show her how to cook them, make pea soup, and store it all for winter," Olivia Owl said.

"I can't wait to give Rebecca Rabbit all the carrots we grew so far. She won't have to eat out of the cans this winter," Bert Bear added.

"It is always good to give to a friend. This is for healthier eating, and it is all the better," Fred Fox explained.

"Let's get all the other vegetables we have grown into the crates and baskets and take them to the farmers' market," Olivia Owl said.

"We can come back and make a delicious pea soup with carrots for dinner tomorrow with Rebecca Rabbit. Maybe she will learn to cook with us this time," Fred Fox suggested. It was now harvest time for the garden they had planted in the spring.

"I can give her the wheelbarrow full of carrots as a surprise," Bert Bear exclaimed.

"It feels like a very organic day for the Organic Animal Club in the garden," Bert Bear stated pleasantly.

The three members of the Organic Animal Club continued their work. They harvested what was ripe bring to the farmers' market. The carrots went straight into the special wheelbarrow for Rebecca Rabbit.

The day was filled with the work to load all the vegetables into the baskets and crates, but the three were full of enthusiasm for the green and organic life.

Bert Bear had arranged for the words" Organic Animal Club" to be painted on the door of the red truck. The back of the truck was loaded with the fresh vegetables. The wheelbarrow full of carrots for Rebecca Rabbit sat waiting by the shed.

CHAPTER 10

The Organic Animals Club Farm Stand

After lots of tender-loving care and work in the garden, the Organic Animal Club's members kept their promise to themselves to sell their vegetables at the farmers' market. The three had worked together in the garden, learning the organic and green ways they wanted to share with others. They had established a small farm business. They had grown and shared sustainable food for themselves and their friend Rebecca Rabbit.

The three friends set up the farm stand at the weekly local farmers' market. It was under a big white tent. The sign under the table announced to everyone that they were the founding members of the Organic Animals Club.

"We did it. We accomplished our goal and have our farm stand at the farmers' market," Bert Bear stated proudly as he set up all the fresh tomatoes and other vegetables.

"We are organic and green now," Fred Fox stated as he looked at all the fresh produce.

"Hopefully, our farm stand continues to be green, not just with the vegetables but also with money that we can reinvest into our garden," Olivia Owl stated with a smile.

"We can share more and make our garden into a large farm someday," Fred Fox stated, dreaming of a green and organic future.

"What a difference from the winter on the couch with junk and processed food. I feel so much healthier and appreciate the earth so much more," Bert Bear declared happily.

The three animals could have easily sold all the carrots they had this week. However, Fred Fox and Bert Bear did not always believe in making a profit. Rather, they believed in making a difference in helping a dear friend like Rebecca Rabbit to eat fewer processed carrots and maybe helping her embrace an organic and green lifestyle.

"Don't forget we are inviting Rebecca Rabbit over for a healthy dinner of pea soup and fresh carrots," Fred Fox stated.

"Customers have been buying so many things today. It is good to see the farmers' market busy," Bert Bear remarked.

Overall, Bert Bear assessed that it was partly economics that Rebecca Rabbit bough processed canned carrots. However, he also thought it was also a bit lazy on Rebecca Rabbit's part for not trying to work in the garden or be the manager at the farm stand. If she did, she may have extra income to buy organic carrots. She would like being outside, being healthy, having her hands in the soil, and cultivating the carrots.

"Someday, she would know what she was missing," thought Bert Bear as he proudly served another customer and packed up the bag of fresh produce.

The farm stand was busy, and the three sold a lot of their vegetables that day. It felt good to display all the fresh produce that they had grown together. It was rewarding to see a demand for the organic vegetables. It was rewarding to see that the customers cared about being green and that most brought their own bags to carry their produce home in.

Bert Bear noticed how happy the customers were to buy locally grown fresh produce. He noticed how good it felt to share the food he and his friends had grown at a relatively modest price. It felt good inside and out to be organic, shop local, and support local farmers.

He wished that he and Fred Fox had shopped more at the farmers' markets instead of eating the pizza, soda, candy, and chips that they had bought at the grocery store all winter. He realized, it was never too late to change his ways and make a new start.

Both were very appreciative of Olivia Owl for sharing her ways with yoga; farmers' markets; and healthy, green, and organic habits. If it were not for Fred Fox taking Bert Bear on the trail hike that day, he would perhaps be sitting on the couch eating candy, drinking soda, and not even feeling energized enough to plant a garden.

Bert Bear could hardly imagine that an inactive, non-green, and non-organic lifestyle was ever his. Once he started to eat right, exercise, and work with his friends, it was as though his entire life had changed for the better. It was never too late to make a change.

At the end of the day, all the farm fresh vegetables had sold, and the three partners packed their baskets and headed home. It had been a good day, and each had a sense of pride about his or her work in the garden. They just wished that Rebecca Rabbit would join them in their club instead of watching them out her kitchen window. They wanted to share the fresh, organic, green life with her.

CHAPTER 11

A Wheelbarrow of Organic Carrots

All summer, Rebecca Rabbit watched Olivia Owl, Bert Bear, and Fred Fox working in the garden. She ate her carrots from the can, stayed out of the sun, and watched them from her window. Sometimes, it made her feel better to be outdoors, but she was not sure why. Olivia Owl told her the sun made everyone grow and happy like a vegetable garden. Maybe it was true.

Fresh vegetables tasted so much better than canned ones. The other ones in the can hardly tasted like carrots compared to the ones the Organic Animal Club grew. There was nothing like the fresh crunch or snap of a fresh organic carrot compared to the ones that had been sitting in the cans for an undetermined amount of time.

That day, she saw her friends harvesting vegetables from the garden for the farm market. After they left, she walked over to see the garden to see what it was all about. It was nice to be outdoors and smell the soil instead of the stuffy air in her house.

"Could it be that fresh air is really good for the mind, body, and soul?" thought Rebecca Rabbit as she stood at the edge of the garden. She walked over to the carrot row and saw that they were all gone. It looked like a lot of work had been done.

She did not really want to work in the garden when she could just go to her cabinet, open the canned carrots, and easily have dinner. She debated whether all the work was worth it. However, she remembered the crisp snap of the fresh carrots as Olivia Owl cut them for the pea soup and how fresh they tasted.

After looking over the garden, she walked near the shed to see what all the watering cans were about. Next to the shed, she saw a wheelbarrow full of carrots just sitting there.

She said to herself, *"Did they leave the carrots behind for a reason? I better taste one and see if there is anything wrong with them."*

She walked over, took one, and ate it. It had the perfect snap of a fresh summer carrot. She admired the bright, gorgeous orange color.

"Maybe these were not up to their standards," she quipped. "Maybe I should take these carrots home with me and make some carrot ginger soup for them as a surprise."

Secretly, Rebecca Rabbit had been reading cookbooks and recipes instead of watching TV and playing video games. She got them at the library and had been trying to learn more because she thought that her friends were perhaps right about being healthy, organic, and green. Maybe it was not such an expensive lifestyle after all. Maybe processed foods cost more in more ways than just money. Maybe they negatively impacted your health in the long run.

She went back into her house, got her big baskets for grocery shopping, and filled them with all the carrots from the wheelbarrow. She took them inside and decided that she would make ginger carrot soup from an organic cookbook she was reading. That was her plan, and the carrots would not go to waste.

CHAPTER 12

The Great Organic Carrot Heist

After returning from the farmers' market, Olivia Owl went to put some supplies back in the toolshed near the garden. It had been a long day, and she wanted to get the fresh carrots to make the pea soup for dinner with Rebecca Rabbit.

She noticed that the wheelbarrow of carrots was empty and looked around the toolshed. There was one carrot on the ground, but the rest was missing. She said, "I think there has been a carrot heist."

She looked around and behind her for clues and could not find any carrots except that one.

"Where did they all go?" asked Olivia Owl.

"Looks like we have an organic mystery to solve," Fred Fox joked.

Bert Bear walked from the red truck back to the garden to get fresh peas, all the while wondering what happened to the carrots he thought he left for Rebecca Rabbit. He looked back at the truck. He specifically left them in the wheelbarrow for Rebecca Rabbit. That was his plan and always had been.

"Well, it looks like there has been a carrot heist of some sort," Bert Bear agreed.

"How are we going to make the pea soup with fresh summer carrots and invite Rebecca Rabbit over now?" asked Olivia Owl, looking puzzled.

"I don't know, and the farmers' market is closed," Fred Fox said.

"Maybe we could ask Rebecca Rabbit for some canned carrots just this once, but I would rather go without them than have canned anything," Bert Bear decided.

"I don't like anything but fresh carrots," Olivia Owl said.

"Maybe she won't mind pea soup without carrots. We can go ask her if that is alright," Bert Bear suggested.

The three of them headed to Rebecca Rabbit's house to ask her to come have pea soup without fresh carrots.

"Plus, maybe Rebecca Rabbit saw something out of her kitchen window today while we were gone," Fred Fox said.

"Maybe. But she usually watches television and plays video games instead of being outdoors," Bert Bear added sadly, remembering when he did that. He felt so much more alive and engaged in life now that he lived green and organic. Everything he did and everything he put into his body mattered. Each vegetable he grew, he cultivated and cared for now.

Things mattered more to him because he saw how vegetables grew in the ground and how they got to his table. He realized how important it was to shop locally and support local businesses.

"Being organic and green has really given me a sense of purpose," Bert Bear admitted proudly to his friends.

"It is a lifestyle for us now and future generations," Fred Fox noted.

"We just have one thing missing from our club, and that is Rebecca Rabbit," Bert Bear said.

"Let's go ask her about the carrots and see if she will ever consider joining our club," Olivia Owl suggested.

The three of them headed off across the grass over to Rebecca Rabbit's house. They were disappointed that they couldn't make the pea soup with carrots for her and show her how to cook it. They really wanted to encourage her to be greener and more organic. Now, they would have to tell her that they would have to make dinner another time after more carrots grew.

"I am most upset that the carrots are gone. I wanted to give them to Rebecca Rabbit to make her life easier and we don't have more to give her from the garden right now" Bert Bear said with despair.

"It will be okay. We can grow more for her," Fred Fox assured him.

Bert Bear sighed heavily and walked with his friends toward Rebecca Rabbit's house.

CHAPTER 13

The Great Organic Carrot Heist Explained

As the three friends came up the path to Rebecca Rabbit's house, they saw her outside dusting off a straw shopping basket. There were still some long fresh greens stuck to it. They looked like carrot tops, but that would not be like her to have fresh carrots around ever.

Bert Bear announced, "All of our fresh organic carrots have been taken from our wheelbarrow."

"Now we can't make the pea soup with carrots for dinner with you," Fred Fox said sadly.

"All of our carrots went missing while we were at the farm stand," Olivia Owl disclosed.

"Did you see anything?" Fred Fox asked quickly.

"Well, I …" Rebecca Rabbit said as she tried to answer.

Bert Bear quickly interrupted her. "Well, we were going to give them all to you to enjoy now and grow more for you for winter."

"Well, I …" Rebecca Rabbit said as she tried to continue.

Suddenly, a gust of wind blew the front door of Rebecca Rabbit's house open. The three friends saw piles of fresh carrots all over the kitchen. They just stared at them and quickly and looked back at Rebecca Rabbit.

"Well, I have carrots and lots of fresh ones. They are actually yours," Rebecca Rabbit said sheepishly.

"Are those the missing carrots from the wheelbarrow?" Bert Bear asked looking in.

"Well, I …" continued Rebecca Rabbit. She was interrupted by Fred Fox this time.

"Olivia Owl was going to show you how to freeze them and store them so you won't have to eat canned carrots anymore," Fred Fox detailed.

All four animals walked inside to Rebecca Rabbit's kitchen. She had a big soup pot full of water on her stove. She had the carrots peeled. Four soup bowls were set on her kitchen table, ready for the soup to be served. Something smelled good. There had never been an aroma of any good sort at Rebecca Rabbit's house. She never cooked anything fresh or organic.

Bert Bear started to sniff the air, and he looked at big soup pot on the stove. It seemed to be warm. Fred Fox smelled something savory and started to smile.

Olivia Owl asked, "Is that a cookbook I see on your kitchen counter?"

"I am sorry. I admit it. I took the carrots from your wheelbarrow. I was going to give them back to you," Rebecca Rabbit said in despair. Her surprise was ruined, but she knew that she should not have taken anything from her friends. For that, she was truly apologetic.

"Give them back to us?" asked Bert Bear.

"As ginger carrot soup from a recipe in this cookbook I got at the library," Rebecca Rabbit said.

"When I saw the wheelbarrow of carrots, I got the idea and thought of my recipe. You worked so hard in the garden today and at the farm stand, and I wanted to do something nice for you," she explained.

"We are not upset. Sharing is caring. We are thrilled that you decided to cook and be organic and green," Olivia Owl said with sincere and utter delight.

"I thought that they had been left behind and that you would not miss them. I thought I could surprise you with a fresh dinner," Rebecca Rabbit said.

She picked up the straw basket bursting with carrots and handed it back to Bert Bear.

"I was going to make some soup and give you some to store for winter in the glass containers I saved all summer long," Rebecca Rabbit said.

"We thought you were inside watching television, but you were reading recipes, recycling, and learning to be green and organic," Fred Fox said with excitement.

"You were at the library reading books about organic life and watching us at the farm stand in the parking lot," said Olivia Owl.

"I grew the carrots for especially for you so that you would not have to eat the processed ones anymore," Bert Bear stated as he touched carrots in the baskets on the table with pride.

"I can see that it is a lot of hard work that pays off with fresh, green, and organic foods. I want to help and join your club," Rebecca Rabbit said.

"We would like that. That way, we can work on the garden more, get more fresh produce, and have healthy long lives," Bert Bear said with a smile.

This was the moment they had all been waiting for. They were thrilled that Rebecca Rabbit wanted to be green and organic. That she wanted to learn to cook and help at the farm stand was a huge bonus for the Organic Animal Club.

"So, there was no great carrot heist after all." said Olivia Owl happily.

"There was a carrot heist that turned into the best green organic day ever, and I hope the soup is just as good," Bert Bear said with a smile.

"Let's turn this into a carrot peeling party and make more soup," proclaimed Fred Fox, happily grabbing a basket of carrots.

"We have one more member of our club now," Olivia Owl said, happily picking up the cookbook to look at the recipe for carrot ginger soup.

"It is never too late to be green or organic," Rebecca Rabbit said.

"It is never too late to eat unprocessed food and be part of the process of being green," Bert Bear agreed. He was very thankful and appreciative that Rebecca Rabbit had turned a green, organic corner.

"A carrot for your thoughts, anyone?" Fred Fox said, smiling at the big pile of baskets on Rebecca Rabbit's table.

It had all come full circle that night. As the Organic Animal Club cooked fresh carrot ginger soup with the formerly doubting Rebecca Rabbit, it seemed as though all of them had found some connection to the green, organic, and healthy lifestyle. It seemed as though there would be a lot more green adventures going forward as they were eating soup that night together.

Sharing truly was caring in the Organic Animal Club. Through educating and informing Rebecca Rabbit about healthy, green, and organic ways, she realized it was right for her. She realized it was right for her health, lifestyle, the planet, and future generations. In small and great ways, everyone can make a difference and make choices that are green and organic and be members of the Organic Animal Club.

Printed in the United States
By Bookmasters